Fire Engines

by Anne E. Hanson

Consultant:
Rob Farmer
Fire Fighter/Paramedic
City of Upper Arlington, Ohio Fire Division

Bridgestone Books
an imprint of Capstone Press
Mankato, Minnesota

Bridgestone Books are published by Capstone Press
151 Good Counsel Drive, P.O. Box 669, Mankato, Minnesota 56002
http://www.capstone-press.com

Library of Congress Cataloging-in-Publication Data
Hanson, Anne E.
    Fire engines/by Anne E. Hanson.
    p. cm.—(The transportation library)
    Includes bibliographical references and index.
    ISBN 0-7368-0842-6
    1. Fire engines—Juvenile literature. [1. Fire engines.] I. Title. II. Series.
TH9372 .H35 2001
628.9'259—dc21   00-009912

Editorial Credits

Karen L. Daas, editor; Karen Risch, product planning editor; Timothy Halldin, cover designer;
    Marilyn LaMantia, illustrator; Heidi Schoof, photo researcher

Photo Credits

Archive Photos, 16
B&W Image Inc./Archive Photos, 14–15
Daniel E. Hodges, cover
DAVID R. FRAZIER Photolibrary, 20
FPG International LLC, 12
Leslie O'Shaughnessy, 8–9
Unicorn Stock Photos/Jean Higgins, 18
Visuals Unlimited/Arthur R. Hill, 4, R. Al Simpson, 6

1 2 3 4 5 6 06 05 04 03 02 01

Table of Contents

Fire Engines

Fire fighters drive fire engines to the scene of a fire. They travel quickly. Fire fighters use fire engines to help put out fires. Fire engines carry water, hoses, and ladders.

Fire Fighters

Fire fighters work to put out fires. They rescue people from burning buildings and cars. They also help people who are hurt. Four to six fire fighters ride on a fire engine. An officer leads the fire fighters on each fire engine.

officer

someone who is in charge of other people

lights

horn

cab

hoses

FIRE • RESCUE

Parts of a Fire Engine

Fire fighters ride in the cab of a fire engine. Sirens, horns, and lights on the cab warn drivers to move out of the way. A tank inside the fire engine holds water. Hoses are on top of the fire engine. Ladders and other tools are on the sides.

hoses

hook ups

engine

How a Fire Engine Works

An engine powers both the fire engine and the water pump. The driver flips a switch after parking the fire engine. The engine then starts pumping water. Fire fighters hook hoses to the pump.

The First Fire Engines

The first fire engines were pumps on carts. People pulled the carts to fires and powered the pumps. The pumps shot a stream of water through a pipe onto the fire. Some pumps had tanks. Others used water from a river or a well.

Early Fire Engines

In the 1800s, fire engines used steam to pump water from a tank. Horses pulled these steam engines to fires. People began to use motor-powered fire engines in the early 1900s.

Fire Engine Rescue Today

Fire engines rush to fires. Some fire fighters carry hoses to the burning building. They shoot water at the fire. Other fire fighters go into the building to help people. Fire fighters provide medical care to those who are injured.

Fire Engine Facts

- Some fire trucks are ladder trucks. Fire fighters use these trucks to reach high places.

- Many fire fighters live at the fire station when they are on duty. They cook meals and sleep there. They can leave quickly when they are called to a fire.

- Dalmatian dogs are pets at some fire stations. Dalmatians ran next to early fire engines. They kept rats and robbers away from the horses.

- Some fires cannot be put out with water. Fire fighters spray foam on these fires.

- In the 1600s, children were fire fighters, too. They passed buckets in the bucket brigades.

Hands On: Flow

Fire fighters need a lot of water to put out a fire. Flow is the amount of water that runs through a fire hose. Fire fighters need enough flow to put out the fire quickly. You can learn about flow.

What You Need

Garden hose
A one-gallon plastic bucket
A stopwatch or a watch with a second hand
A friend

What You Do

1. Turn on the water at full force.
2. Fill the bucket with water. Have your friend empty the bucket when it is full. Do this for one minute. How many buckets can you fill?
3. Turn the water down. Repeat step 2.

You can fill the bucket faster when more water flows through the hose. Water flows through fire hoses at as much as 400 gallons (1,500 liters) per minute. Most fire engines hold about 1,250 gallons (4,700 liters) of water. They get more water from fire hydrants.

Words to Know

brigade (bri-GAYD)—an organized group of workers

engine (EN-juhn)—a machine that makes the power needed to move something

foam (FOHM)—a mixture of bubbles used to put out fires

officer (OF-uh-sur)—someone who is in charge of other people

pump (PUHMP)—a machine that forces water or foam through a hose

Read More

Budd, E. S. *Fire Engines.* Rescue Machines at Work. Eden Prairie, Minn.: Child's World, 1999.

Otfinoski, Steve. *To the Rescue: Fire Trucks Then and Now.* Here We Go! Tarrytown, N.Y.: Benchmark Books, 1997.

Ready, Dee. *Fire Fighters.* Community Helpers. Mankato, Minn.: Bridgestone Books, 1997.

Internet Sites

Fire Administration Kids Page
http://www.usfa.fema.gov/kids
Fire Safety for Kids
http://www.dos.state.ny.us/kidsroom/firesafe/firesafe.html
Sparky the Fire Dog
http://www.sparky.org

Index